Katie Woo's

✳ Neighborhood ✳

Nurse Kenji Rules!

D0032185

by Fran Manushkin

illustrated by Laura Zarrin

WINDOW BOOKS
tone imprint

Katie Woo's Neighborhood is published by
Picture Window Books, an imprint of Capstone.
1710 Roe Crest Drive
North Mankato, Minnesota 56003
www.capstonepub.com

Text © 2021 Fran Manushkin
Illustrations © 2021 Picture Window Books

Library of Congress Cataloging-in-Publication Data
Names: Manushkin, Fran, author. | Zarrin, Laura, illustrator.
Title: Nurse Kenji rules! / by Fran Manushkin ; illustrated by Laura Zarrin.
Description: North Mankato, Minnesota : Picture Window Books, a Capstone imprint, [2021] | Series: Katie Woo's neighborhood | Audience: Ages 5-7. | Audience: Grades K-1. |
Summary: Katie Woo and her parents help their new neighbor, Mr. Kenji, to prepare for his final test to become a nurse.
Identifiers: LCCN 2020035171 (print) | LCCN 2020035172 (ebook) | ISBN 9781515882428 (hardcover) | ISBN 9781515883517 (paperback) | ISBN 9781515892144 (pdf) | ISBN 9781515893059 (kindle edition)
Subjects: CYAC: Nurses—Fiction. | Examinations—Fiction. | Chinese Americans—Fiction.
Classification: LCC PZ7.M3195 Nur 2021 (print) | LCC PZ7.M3195 (ebook) | DDC [E]—dc23
LC record available at https://lccn.loc.gov/2020035171
LC ebook record available at https://lccn.loc.gov/2020035172

Designer: Bobbie Nuytten

Printed and bound in the USA. PO 3837

Table of Contents

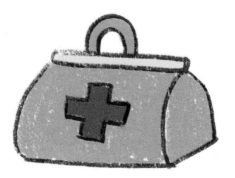

Katie's Neighborhood

Police

Library

Mechanic

Grocery Store

City Hall

Post Office

School

Chapter 1
Worried Mr. Kenji

Katie had a new neighbor.

His name was Mr. Kenji.

He loved his garden, and he

loved taking photos of his

family.

One day, Mr. Kenji looked worried. He told Katie's mom, "I want to be a nurse, and my final test is next week. I hope I pass it!"

"We can help," said Katie.

"Let's pretend that I am sick.
You can be my nurse. Mom
and Dad will decide if you
are doing a good job!"

Chapter 2

Pretending and Practicing

Mr. Kenji came into

their house. He washed his

hands. Then he asked Katie,

"What's wrong? Why did

you call me?"

Katie made a sad face.

"I am feeling sick. Everything

hurts."

"I'm sorry to hear that,"

said Mr. Kenji. "I will try to

help you."

"First, I will take your temperature," said Mr. Kenji. He looked at his thermometer. "You do not have a fever. That's good!"

"But my heart is beating very fast!" said Katie "Maybe you should check it."

"I always do that," said Mr. Kenji.

"I will use this stethoscope," said Mr. Kenji.

"Wow!" said Katie. "That's a big word."

"It has to do a big job," said Mr. Kenji. "Your heart is very important."

"Your heart sounds fine," said Mr. Kenji. "It's not beating too fast."

"Can I listen?" asked Katie.

"Oh my!" Katie smiled. "My heart is awesome."

Katie asked Mr. Kenji,

"Can I listen to *your* heart?"

She heard: *Poom POOM!*

Poom POOM! Poom POOM!

Katie's mom listened too.

She said. "It is beating very

fast."

"I think you are still
worried about your test,"
said Katie's mom. "Let me
make you a cup of tea.
Drinking tea always makes
me feel calmer."

Katie's mom poured the tea. Oops! She spilled hot water on her hand.

"*Ouch!*" she yelled.

"It hurts."

"I can help you," said

Mr. Kenji. He washed her

hand in cool water. He put

on ointment and a bandage.

"Now it will heal."

"Thank you!" said Katie's

mom.

Suddenly, Katie's dad lay down on the couch.

"Something is wrong," he gasped. "I can't breathe! My throat and my chest hurt."

Mr. Kenji stayed calm. He took Mr. Woo's temperature. He checked his throat and his chest and his heart.

"Nothing is wrong," he said. "You are fine!"

"That's right! I am!"

Mr. Woo jumped up. "I

wanted to see if you were

calm in a crisis. You passed."

Katie laughed. "Wow, Dad! You are great at playing pretend."

Mr. Kenji smiled too. "This practice was great! I feel better about taking my test."

Chapter 3

Nurse Kenji

Two weeks later,

Mr. Kenji took his test.

He stayed calm and smart.

He got a terrific grade.

Oh, was he happy!

He told Katie and her
mom and dad, "You helped
me so much!"

Mr. Kenji had a party
with his family and his
friends. It was a great
celebration.

Everyone felt terrific!

Glossary

bandage (BAN-dij)—a covering that protects wounds

breathe (BREETH)—to take air in and out of the lungs

celebration (sel-uh-BRAY-shuhn)—a special gathering

fever (FEE-ver)—a rise in body temperature that sometimes means you are sick

ointment (OINT-muhnt)—an oily medicine used on skin

stethoscope (STETH-uh-skohp)—a tool used to listen to the heart and lungs

temperature (TEM-pur-uh-chur)—the measure of how hot or cold something is

thermometer (thur-MOM-uh-tur)—a tool that measures temperature

Katie's Questions

1. What traits make a good nurse? Would you like to be a nurse? Why or why not?

2. What nursing tools did Mr. Kenji use in the story? Write a list. Can you think of any other tools a nurse might use?

3. Mr. Kenji felt nervous about his test. What things did the Woo family do to make him feel better?

4. Does your school have a nurse? Write a paragraph about him or her and draw a picture to go with it.

5. Pretend you are going to Nurse Kenji's party. Make him a card to say congratulations. Write him a special message.

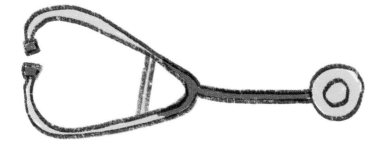

Katie Interviews a Nurse

Katie: Hi, Nurse Kenji! I love calling you that since you are officially a nurse!
Nurse Kenji: And I love hearing it! Thank you for all the help you gave me when I was preparing for my test.

Katie: What is your favorite part about your job?
Nurse Kenji: I work in a doctor's office. The doctor I work with treats patients of all ages. I like working with the kids best. Sometimes kids are nervous when they go to the doctor. I like to tell them jokes so they feel more relaxed.

Katie: You work in a doctor's office, but nurses work other places too. Where are some of those places?
Nurse Kenji: Some of my classmates found jobs working with elderly people at nursing homes. Others go to patients' homes and care for them there. And many of them work in hospitals.

Katie: Hospitals need lots of nurses! Would you want to work at a hospital some day?

Nurse Kenji: I think I might. Hospital nurses work long hours—ten to twelve hours a day! But there are lots of different nursing jobs in a hospital. You could work in the emergency room or help deliver babies. You could work with heart patients. Or you might work in the ICU. That's where the sickest patients stay.

Katie: Tell me about what you wear to work, Nurse Kenji.

Nurse Kenji: Nurses wear outfits called scrubs. They are sturdy and can be washed with a strong soap to kill germs. I also wear comfortable shoes because I'm on my feet a lot.

Katie: Well, thanks again for taking the time to talk to me.

Nurse Kenji: And thank you again for helping me study for the test. You are a good neighbor, Katie!

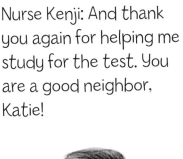

About the Author

Fran Manushkin is the author of Katie Woo, the highly acclaimed fan-favorite early reader series, as well as the popular Pedro series. Her other books include *Happy in Our Skin*, *Baby, Come Out!* and the best-selling board books *Big Girl Panties* and *Big Boy Underpants*. There is a real Katie Woo: Fran's great-niece, who doesn't get into trouble like the Katie in the books. Fran lives in New York City, three blocks from Central Park, where she can often be found bird-watching and daydreaming. She writes at her dining room table, without the help of her two naughty cats, Chaim and Goldy.

About the Illustrator

Laura Zarrin spent her early childhood in the St. Louis, Missouri, area. There she explored creeks, woods, and attic closets, climbed trees, and dug for artifacts in the backyard, all in preparation for her future career as an archaeologist. She never became one, however, because she realized she's much happier drawing in the comfort of her own home while watching TV. When she was twelve, her family moved to the Silicon Valley in California, where she still lives with her very logical husband and teen sons, and their illogical dog, Cody.